Who Laid Tho???? ????s?

Written by G. Petreman   Photos by G. Petreman & K. Mancuso

A special thanks to Erich Jacoby-Hawkins
for his contributions and James Krant for his photo of the blue jay

Order this book online at www.trafford.com
or email orders@trafford.com

Most Trafford titles are also available at major online book retailers.

Printed in the United States of America.

ISBN: 978-1-4669-7633-7 (sc)

978-1-4669-7632-0 (e)

Trafford rev. 04/27/2013

 www.trafford.com

North America & international
toll-free: 1 888 232 4444 (USA & Canada)
phone: 250 383 6864 ♦ fax: 812 355 4082

Twins Bryanna and Ryan were sad. Their mom and dad were getting a divorce. Their mom was moving into a condo. Their dad was moving away to a new job. They would be spending most of their time with their mom in her new condo.

"It's not fair! I love birds! I love feeding chickadees and goldfinches! I won't see any birds way up on the 7th floor!" cried Bryanna.

Their mom promised to take them shopping to buy flowers and garden ornaments for the balcony.

After they returned from the garden center, they placed a small table, chairs, a shelf, and planters on the balcony for Bryanna's favorite flowers. The next day, when Bryanna went out on the balcony to plant some more flowers she immediately rushed inside.

"Mom! Mom! Come quick," she shrieked.

Bryanna's mom rushed out onto the balcony.

"Mom! How did they get here? Who laid those eggs?" asked Bryanna as she pointed to two plain-looking white eggs resting in a poorly constructed nest inside her pail planter.

"I don't know! But we need to leave the balcony quickly, so the mother bird will come back and keep them warm! If the eggs get too cold, the baby chicks will die!" explained their mom.

Once inside, Ryan arrived with a pail full of his favorite rocks. "I'm going to put out my stone frog with my rock collection," he declared as he headed towards the balcony door.

"Stop! You can't go out on the balcony!" yelled Bryanna.

"You're not the boss of me!" cried Ryan.

When his mom explained to him about their discovery he became quite excited.

"Maybe, it's a bald eagle! I think bald eagles are cool! Mom, may I use your camera to take a picture of the eggs?" asked Ryan.

Ryan returned from the balcony almost immediately.

"That was fast! Did you get a good picture?" asked his mom.

"No! I couldn't! Come look!" whispered Ryan.

There in the middle of the planter sat a good-sized bird with a small head and a pointed tail with black-bordered white tips. Its feathers were mostly a delicate brown. As they stood and stared at the bird it did not move except for the occasional blinking of its eyes.

"What kind of bird is that?" asked Bryanna in a quiet voice.

"It's a mourning dove!" replied their mom.

"I think it must be the mother. Look at the patches of pink feathers on its neck. And its throat is pink-looking too!" cried Bryanna.

"Believe it or not, it is actually a male bird. The father sits on the eggs most of the day. Then the mother arrives in the afternoon and keeps the eggs warm until the next morning when the father returns," explained their mom.

After lunch the twins and their mother went to the local library to borrow some bird books.

Every day for 13 days, Ryan took photos of the doves and Bryanna wrote about them in her notebook. On the 14th day, as Ryan was taking some photos, he began to shout in a loud voice.

"Bryanna! Come look!"

Ryan snapped several photos of the sight that appeared before him. A tiny head, two bulging eyes, a big beak, and scaly-looking feathers were peeking out from under the mourning dove.

Mom explained to the twins that one of the eggs hatches on one day and the second egg hatches the day after.

For the next few days Bryanna and Ryan continually checked on the mourning doves to catch the mom or dad feeding them. But they never did! They began to worry that the babies would starve to death.

They started to read their bird books. First of all, they discovered that baby mourning doves were not called chicks, but were actually called squabs.

Their mom asked Ryan to read from the bird book.

In a clear and confident voice Ryan read, **"Both parents feed the squabs. The parent opens its mouth wide and the squab sticks its head inside to feed on the nutritious food called pigeon milk. Rich in protein and fat it looks like cottage cheese. By the fourth day the parents add seeds to the squabs' diet as well."**

"Oh, that explains why we never see the squabs with their beaks wide open, waiting for bugs to be dropped down their throats!" cried Ryan.

As the baby squabs got bigger, they had a hard time keeping warm as they protruded out from under the wings of their parents. It was still March. Often the days and especially the nights were quite cool.

As the days passed Ryan noticed something quite unusual on the mourning doves.

"It looks like the doves are growing a skirt of baby blue feathers to keep the squabs warm!" pointed out Bryanna.

"I'm not sure about that! I know that mourning doves have lots of fluffy, downy feathers that might look like a skirt. You'll have to ask your teacher to study that at school," replied their mom.

About 2 weeks after the eggs had hatched, Bryanna and Ryan were met with a surprise. The two squabs with their dark, scaly feathers, small heads, and pointed tails were cuddled side by side. There was no father or mother bird in sight!

"What happened to their mom and dad? Why aren't they keeping the babies warm? They are going to freeze when night comes!" cried Bryanna in a worried voice.

In the afternoon when the twins returned from school the two baby squabs were still all alone.

All afternoon the twins checked on the birds. Just as the sun was setting the twins heard a soft, "Coo! Coo!" There, sitting on the edge of the balcony, was one of the mourning doves. It just sat on the balcony railing and cooed. As the twins watched, suddenly one of the squabs started to stand up. It began flapping its wings, and before the twins had a chance to save it, the squab tumbled to the concrete floor, and disappeared over the edge of the balcony.

"Oh no! It's going to get killed!" screeched the twins as they raced toward the edge.

They could not believe their eyes! The squab was flapping its wings gracefully and confidently as it flew toward some trees.

The twins looked at the nest to see if the other squab was going to fly away too. But, like a stone, it sat silently on its nest. All night and all the next day the remaining squab sat in silence, without moving.

The next evening the twins watched and waited for the mother to return. But she never came back.

Then to their surprise the squab slowly started to move. First it stood up, then it looked around and before they could call their mom, it flapped its wings and flew gracefully in the same direction as the other squab.

The next day the twins informed their mom that they missed the doves.

"Guess what I just read from the bird book we got from the library? Here Bryanna read what it says," beamed their mom.

In a loud and clear voice Bryanna read, *"Mourning doves have been known to reuse the same nest for five sets of eggs in a single season."*

"That means they're coming back!" yelled Bryanna, "I'm going to make a great nest for them starting right now."

"Can I help?" asked Ryan.

"Of course you can! Go outside and find some twigs and I'm going to get some pretty yarn and ribbons," cried Bryanna.

Ryan and Bryanna's Questions About Birds

❖ 1. How many different kinds of birds are there on Earth?

❖ 2. How can you help birds to survive?

❖ 3. What do birds have that no other animal has?

❖ 4. Are birds helpful or harmful?

❖ 5. Why do some birds migrate?

❖ 6. Which bird lives the longest?

❖ 7. Which bird is the most dangerous?

❖ 8. Do all birds have wings?

❖ 9. Do all birds know how to fly?

❖ 10. Which bird is the fastest flyer?

❖ 11. Which bird has the longest feathers?

❖ 12. Which bird has the most feathers?

❖ 13. Which bird has the longest beak?

❖ 14. Which bird is the most intelligent?

❖ 15. Which bird is the fastest swimmer?

❖ 16. Which bird can stay under water the longest?

❖ 17. Which bird can go without food the longest?

❖ 18. Which bird is known as an incredible thief?

How Many Did You Get Correct?

❖ 1. There are about 9 000 species of birds.

❖ 2. You can help birds to survive by planting trees. Trees provide food, dew, shelter, nesting materials, and resting and observation points for birds. Trees also help reduce the devastating effects of climate change such as droughts and flooding. Not only do birds benefit from a dense covering of trees, but people do as well. Trees help purify the air by trapping dirt, dust, and nasty pollutants.

❖ 3. Birds are the only animals on Earth that have feathers.

❖ 4. Birds can be both helpful and harmful. They are helpful when they eat harmful insect and weed seeds. Predatory birds such as the owl, hawk, and eagle keep down the populations of rats, mice, and other rodents that eat our crops. Birds also help pollinate many flowering plants. Seeds that birds eat are passed through their bodies and fall to the ground and plants begin to grow in new areas. Domestic birds such as the chicken, turkey, duck, and goose give us meat and eggs. We use feathers to stuff pillows, quilts, and outdoor clothing.
   Birds are harmful when they eat crops and kill farm animals and pets.

❖ 5. Many birds migrate south when they can no longer find food.

❖ 6. Among the longest-living birds are **parrots**. Various species of **parrots** can live from 40 to over 100 years.

❖ 7. According to the Guinness Book of World Records, the **cassowary** is the world's most dangerous bird! The **cassowary** lives in the rainforests of Australia and New Guinea. It is dangerous, aggressive, and unpredictable! The powerful force of its kick has been known to break bones and even kill. Its dagger-like sharp claws can deliver a serious injury.

❖ 8. All birds have wings. The **kiwi** bird of New Zealand appears to have none, but they have tiny wings hidden under their hairy feathers.

❖ 9. The **kiwi** and **kakapo parrot** of New Zealand, the **emu** and the **cassowary** of Australia, the **rhea** of South America, the **tinamous** from Central and South America, the **ostrich**, and the **penguin** cannot fly.

❖ 10. When diving for prey, the **peregrine falcon** can reach speeds over 320 kilometers per hour (over 200 miles per hour)!

❖ 11. The **onagadori**, a domestic strain of the **red jungle fowl**, can have feathers as long as 9–10 meters (more than 30 feet).

❖ 12. A **whistling swan** can have up to 25 000 feathers!

❖ 13. The **Australian pelican's** beak can grow to be 47 centimeters long (18.5inches).

❖ 14. **African gray parrots** and **crows** are considered to be the most intelligent. The **African gray parrot** can learn to count, identify objects, shapes, colors, and materials. Some can learn a vocabulary of about 800 words!

❖ 15. **Gentoo Penguins** from the Antarctic Islands are the fastest-swimming birds.

❖ 16. **The emperor penguin** can stay underwater up to 18 minutes!

❖ 17. A male **emperor penguin** goes without food for 134 days while it incubates its egg! The female lays only one egg.

❖ 18. The **magpie** collects shiny objects for its nest. It will steal anything shiny, even jewelry. It is known as the "**The Thieving Magpie**".

Black-capped Chickadee

Blue Jay

Common Loon

Red-breasted Nuthatch

American Goldfinch

Great Blue Heron

Canada Goose

Yellow Warbler

There are about 9 000 species of birds.

Red-eyed Vireo

Palm Warbler

Sharp-shinned Hawk

Mallard Duckling

Turkey Poult

Hairy Woodpecker

Yellow-bellied Sapsucker

Yellow-rumped Warbler